MICKEY'S PERFECTO DAY!

Adapted by **Sherri Stoner**

Based on the episode written by **Ashley Mendoza**

Illustrated by **Loter, Inc.**

DISNEP PRESS

Los Angeles • New York

First Paperback Edition, October 2017 10 9 8 7 6 5 4 3 2 1
ISBN 978-1-368-01028-3
FAC-029261-17258
Library of Congress Control Number: 2017947683

Printed in the United States of America
For more Disney Press fun, visit www.disneybooks.com

SUSTAINABLE
FORESTRY
INITIATIVE

Certified Chain of Custody
Promoting Sustainable Forestry

www.sfiprogram.org
SFI-01415

The SFI label applies to the text stock

Mickey and his pals pack for a trip.
They are going to Madrid, Spain.
They will see the sights.
Donald will sing with his friends.
It will be a *perfecto* day!

The gang drives their Daily Drivers
to Madrid.

They pass a baby bull sniffing a rose.
The rose falls off the bush.
It lands in Minnie's car!

Minnie puts the rose behind her ear.
The baby bull runs after his rose.
Minnie does not notice.

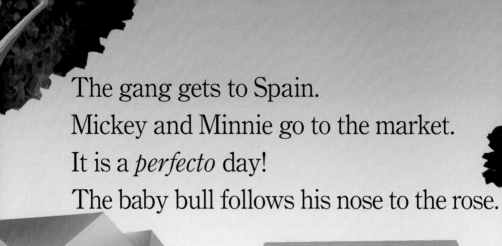

The gang gets to Spain.

Mickey and Minnie go to the market.

It is a *perfecto* day!

The baby bull follows his nose to the rose.

Minnie shops.

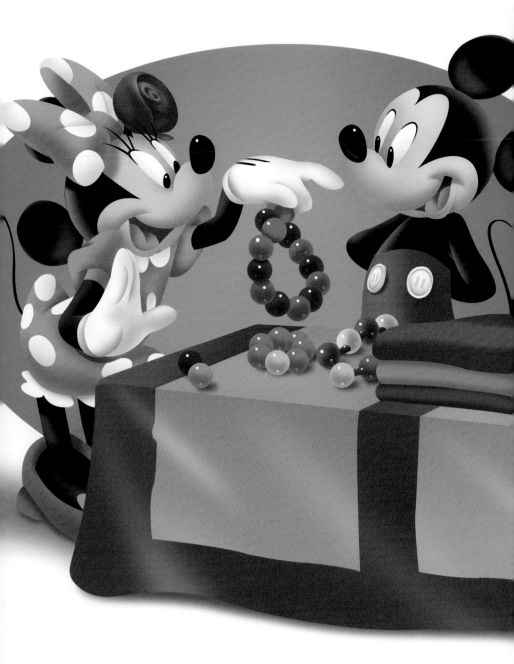

Minnie tries on dresses.

The baby bull sniffs the rose.

Minnie does not notice.

But Mickey notices!
"B-b-b-bull!" Mickey shouts.

Mickey and Minnie jump into a cart.
It rolls away from the bull.
It rolls into . . .

. . . a churro cart!
"We'll take two," says Mickey.

Donald finds his friends.
They invite Daisy and Donald to lunch.
It is a *perfecto* day!

Donald tries the potatoes.
"AAAACK!" he shouts.
They are very spicy.

Daisy tries to help.
She gives him water to drink.

It's almost time to sing.
The group warms up.
Donald opens his mouth.
No sound comes out.

Who will sing at the show?
Donald's friends ask Daisy to sing!

Donald is sad he can't sing with
his friends.
He gives Daisy his hat.

Poor Donald.

His friend brings him dessert.

He will watch the show from his table.

Mickey and Minnie visit the plaza.
The bull visits the plaza, too.

He follows his nose to the rose.
Mickey and Minnie run!

The friends find a spot to hide in.
The baby bull runs right by them.

Mickey and Minnie run to the show.
Daisy is singing with the band.

Donald finishes dessert.
He gets the bill.
"WHAT?" he shouts.
His voice is back!

Donald joins the band.
They sing together.
The crowd loves the show!

The baby bull comes to the show, too.
He sits next to Minnie.
He sniffs her rose.

"He just likes my flower!" Minnie says.
She gives the bull her rose.
The bull gives Mickey a kiss!

Minnie giggles.
What a *perfecto* day!